Snow White
and the Seven Dwarfs

Book One

DISNEY PRESS
New York • Los Angeles

Once upon a time, in a faraway land, there lived a beautiful princess named Snow White. Snow White's stepmother, the Queen, was a vain woman. She hated anyone whose beauty rivaled her own. And so she dressed Snow White in rags and forced her to clean and scrub the castle.

Each day, the Queen asked her magic mirror, "Magic Mirror on the wall, who is the fairest one of all?"

And each day the mirror replied, "You are the fairest one of all."

Then one afternoon, the Queen asked, "Magic Mirror on the wall, who is the fairest one of all?"

But this time the mirror replied, "Snow White."

Pale with anger, the Queen summoned the Huntsman. "Take Snow White deep into the forest and bring me back her heart!" she commanded.

The Huntsman bowed his head. He had no choice but to obey.

The Huntsman led Snow White into the forest. But he could not bring himself to harm her.

"Run away!" the Huntsman said. "Hide, and never come back."

Scared, Snow White fled through the forest. At last, she fell down wearily to the ground and began to cry.

When Snow White dried her eyes, she found a group of friendly animals watching her. The gentle creatures listened to Snow White's sad story, then quickly led her to a charming little cottage.

"It's just like a doll's house!" she exclaimed.

The princess knocked on the door. When there was no answer, she let herself in.

Inside the cozy cottage, Snow White found a long wooden table and seven tiny chairs. "There must be seven children living here," she said. "Seven untidy children," she added, looking at the dust and cobwebs all around her.

Suddenly, Snow White had an idea. "If we clean the place up," she told her animal friends, "perhaps they'll let me stay!"

When the room was clean as could be, Snow White went off to explore the rest of the cottage.

Upstairs, Snow White found a big room with seven little beds.

"These beds do look quite comfortable," Snow White said.

Yawning, she sank down across the beds and was soon asleep.

That night, the owners of the cottage returned. But they weren't seven little children—they were the Seven Dwarfs! When the Dwarfs saw their clean and tidy house, they knew something strange was going on.

The Seven Dwarfs crept upstairs and found Snow White stretching and yawning under the sheets. As they peered over the beds at the princess, she woke up.

"How do you do?" she said.

Snow White told the Dwarfs her sad story, and they agreed to let her stay with them.

"We'll protect you from the Queen," they told Snow White.

Snow White set to work at once making dinner for the Dwarfs. Before she would let them eat, she insisted that they wash up.

"Wash!" cried the little men. But Snow White just showed them to the tub.

That evening, Snow White and the Seven Dwarfs sang and danced into the wee hours. Snow White felt safe and protected in the little cottage.

Before they went to sleep, Snow White told the Dwarfs a bedtime story—all about the handsome prince of her dreams.

Meanwhile, at the castle, the evil Queen had learned from her magic mirror that Snow White was still alive. She decided to get rid of the girl once and for all.

Calling upon her evil powers, the Queen made a potion that would transform her into an ugly old hag.

Then, using her book of magic, the Queen created a poison apple.

"One taste and Snow White's eyes will close forever!" she cackled.

There was only one cure for the Queen's sleeping spell—love's first kiss.

The next morning, Snow White gave each Dwarf a kiss on the head and then sent them off to work in the diamond mines.

"Beware of strangers," the Dwarfs warned. Then they marched off, cheerfully singing, "Heigh-ho, heigh-ho! It's off to work we go!"

As Snow White began her chores, an old beggar woman suddenly appeared.

"Making pies, dearie?" she asked. "It's apple pies the men love. Here, taste one of these." She held out a big red apple.

Snow White remembered the Dwarfs' warning. But the woman seemed harmless, and the apple *did* look delicious.

Snow White invited the beggar woman inside. Once again, the woman offered Snow White the apple.

"This is a magic wishing apple," the old woman continued. "One bite and all your dreams will come true."

Snow White, who knew a lot about dreams but little of evil, reached for the apple and took a bite. Then, with a sigh, she fell to the floor.

Snow White's animal friends raced off to find the Dwarfs.

The Dwarfs arrived at the cottage just as the old hag, who was really the Queen, was leaving. They chased her through the woods and up a rocky cliff. Higher and higher she climbed, with the Dwarfs close behind. Lightning crashed and thunder boomed. Suddenly, the hag lost her footing. With a shriek, she fell off the cliff to her doom.

The evil Queen was gone, but the Dwarfs were too late to save Snow White. The Dwarfs, who had grown to love their princess, could not bear to part with her. And so they built her a coffin of glass and gold and vowed to keep watch over her day and night.